TRITTA

A THE NEXT STEP TALE

Brittany

I sit in bed in my underwear
scrolling through Instagram.
Honestly, I wish people would stop
rambling on about Trevor and I.
I love being an actress and having
fans but the lack of privacy aspect
isn't so good. Ok so Trevor and I love

each other and we're a happily married couple but I wish that my love life wasn't posted all over the Internet! But I can't really complain, I chose this and I'm happy with life!

"Trevor!" I call.

"Yeah, babe?!" he answers.

"The internet is just so...." I search for a word but he beats me to it.

"I know babe but it's our life that we chose!" he says in a muffled voice, walking through from the bathroom in his boxers, brushing his teeth.

"Yeah, I guess." I say.

Just then our toddler, Riley runs through and tries to climb onto the bed. She's 2 years old and very adventurous. Trevor lifts her up and I hug her to my breast. "Now, How on earth did you get out of your crib?" I ask surprised. She looks up at me and giggles.

"Mommy, I Riley!" she says proudly. Her first words were: 'I', 'Riley',

'Daddy' and 'Mommy'. So now she goes around saying:

'mommy/daddy, 1 Riley!'. It's really sweet.

"Yes sweetie, you're Riley!" 1 tell her as 1 kiss the top of her head.

"Come on! Lets go and get ready while daddy gets ready too!" 1 say to her. Then 1 take her hand and lead her through to her room and 1 look through the drawers for some clothes for her to wear. 1 eventually produce a gorgeous fluffy topped dress with a flower pattern at the bottom, in lovely cream colors. I dress her in it, along with cream pumps. Then I tie her silky short brown hair up in two little pigtails. She looks gorgeous as always. I give her a kiss on her red little lips as she dances around the room and then walk back into Trevor and my room. Trevor is lying fully dressed on the bed with his cute little black quiff of hair at the front perfectly styled, as usual, texting on his phone. I choose my outfit, a loose grey strap top with black jeans and silver sandals. Then I curl my dyed smoky blonde hair and apply some peach lip-stick, concealer, mascara, eye liner, eyebrow pencil and dark grey eye shadow. Today we're going to a TNS fan 'meet n' greet'.

The Next Step finally ended a few months ago now, but the fans still love concerts and meet n' greets.

Victoria, Alexandra and Lamar

should be there too! Lamar really

loves Riley and Riley really loves

Lamar! They seem to get along,

perhaps...

I close the window where the soft

autumn breeze is wafting through.

Trevor goes to get Riley while I get

our coats. I help Riley put on her

little pink, white and purple flowery

raincoat while Trevor slides on his

black cashmere duffel. Then I pull on my short black cardigan and grab my bag, keys and phone. We all leave through the front door of our gorgeous Canadian villa and I carry Riley. Then we go to the car and I buckle Riley into her car seat. Then Trevor and I get in and begin driving to downtown Toronto. When we arrive there's a long strip of fans waving and smiling and holding signs. I carry Riley as we wave, she waves excitedly, she's such an attention seeker, just like me! Sometimes Riley's a nightmare dressed as a daydream! When we get inside the private area I let Riley run off, and I know she's searching for Lamar. Trevor follows her. She's been to a few meet n' greets now but she always stays in the private staff lounge with Sally, Alex's nice assistant. I spot Victoria and walk over. "Vic!" I shout excitedly.

"BRIT! OH MY WORD!" she shouts back. We hug and smile. Vic's probably my best-est friend from the show, but I have loads so its hard to choose!

"How's Brandon?" I ask. Brandon is Victoria's one-year boyfriend.

"Oh! Guess what! We're engaged!" she tells me happily.

"OH MY WORD! VIC! HOW LONG?" I scream excitedly.

"A week!" she tells me as we hug again. Then Lamar (holding Riley in his arms), Alexandra and Trevor come through, wondering what all the commotion is about. I nod at Vic to tell them, take Riley from Lamar and stand next to Trevor as he slings his arm around me.

"Well everyone, I have some news......Brandon and I are engaged!" she tells them excitedly. They all hug and congratulate her.

Then I take Riley through to the

private lounge and give her to Sally.

Trevor

Eventually it's time to go and meet the fans. Brittany and I give Riley a kiss then go to meet them. We sit in the chairs and wave at the long queue. As they come one by one they ask us questions, take pictures and we sign autographs. Eventually, a little girl comes up to Brittany and she asks "When is Riley coming out? I want a picture with her!" Brittany and I glance at each other nervously. "Well....Riley doesn't come o......" I begin but never get to finish as the whole line of people must have overheard as they start chanting 'Riley! Riley!'. We try to calm them down but they are chanting it louder and louder. Suddenly, Riley runs out the back private door with Sally running closely behind looking worried, she must have heard her name being called. Everyone claps when they see her and Riley waves proudly back. Brittany rushes over and picks her up then shifts Riley to sit on her hip. I stand next to them with my arm round Brittany as we all look anxiously at the crowd, who are all taking pictures. Brittany occasionally lets Riley be on social media but she doesn't want her to be all over the internet. She knows she can't protect Riley from everything but she doesn't want her shown everywhere and I agree. We quickly run through the back private door with Riley in Brit's arms and decide that one of us needs to sit with her. Brittany volunteers. She signs a few quick autographs then goes back to Riley. I sit and keep signing autos.

Brittany

I sit in the lounge with a steaming *Starbucks* coffee (my favourite!). Meanwhile Riley plays with her white fluffy toy bunny (from my sister, Sam) on the floor. Frank comes through half an hour later and sits next to me, I know what he's about to say isn't good.

"Brittany, why aren't you out there with the fans?" he says in frustrated tones, then sighs. "I need to be in here with Riley! I'm sorry Frank, but she comes before the show!" I tell him a little angrily, "I thought I made that clear when she was born!" I add.

"Brittany, I know we finished filming the whole show a while ago but I still need your 100% put into the fans!" He tells me furiously.

"WELL, YOU KNOW WHAT? I'M DONE!" I shoot back. Then I gather up Riley's things take her hand and leave, not looking back, as Frank looks at me stunned. Riley pulls at my top and I stop, crouch down and look at her. "What, honey?" I ask concerned,

"Where daddy? Want daddy!" she says as she starts crying.

"Sweetie, daddy is coming soon." I say as I get a tissue and wipe her eyes. Then I take her hand and we begin walking. I text Trevor as we

do:
Babe, going home with Riley.
Love u! Bxx

A moment later a text appears back

from him:
Ok, u ok? Almost done! Talk to u later.
Love u! Txx

I frown then slide my phone back in

my pocket.

"Come on Riles, lets go home." I say.

Then I buckle up Riley, get in the car

and we drive home. When we get

home I put Riley to bed in her crib

in her room, then I'm so tired I have a bath, change into Trev's shirt then slide into our fresh crisp bed. When I wake Trevor is stroking my cheek and we lean in and kiss.

"Want to tell me what happened earlier?" He asks.

"Yes, but let me get changed first, Vic's coming for dinner in 3 hours." I say as I check the time. I slide out of bed, pull of Trevor's shirt that I was wearing and dump it on the floor. Trevor grabs my arm just as I'm going into the bathroom. I turn to face him and then, I don't know how but we're kissing. I have my hands on his strong cheeks and he has his hands on my tanned smooth bare waist. I'm standing on my tippy toes, as he's too tall. Then the moment is broken as Riley cries. "I'll get her" says Trevor and leaves the room. I pull on a light brown long sleeved top and a light brown,

light cream and black tartan skirt.
Then some white knee high socks
and brown ankle boots. And throw
on a matching tartan scarf. I then
redo my makeup and curl my dyed
smoky blonde hair again. Then I go
through to Riley's room to find
Trevor sitting on the chair, with
Riley on his knee, reading a story to
her as she points at the pictures. I
smile and get out my phone, take a
picture then post it on instagram.

It's so sweet! I then join them. It's the perfect family moment! Afterwards I leave them to it and with the dinner cooking I settle down with a mug of coffee and cross my legs as I look at our wedding album. Then Trevor comes back down.

"Honey, Riley's asleep. Want to tell me what happened earlier?" He says gently.

I sigh and make him a coffee, hand it to him, then sit back down and begin..... "Well," I inhale sharply, "just after 'The Riley Scene' today Frank walked in and said how I needed to be 100% committed to the fans. I just said that I'd made it clear when Riley was born that family came first. But that kinda backfired because I got all worked up and quit..." I say, getting all worked up again.

I stop as I see Trevor's stunned face.

"Wait let me get this straight!... You quit?!" He asks, surprised.

"Yes, are you mad with me?" I ask as I look at him nervously.

"No, honey! Of course not! That's your decision and I think it's better for you to be home with Riley." He says, like the funny supportive young husband he is.

"Thanks honey." I say and we lean in to kiss as he pulls my chin close to his lips. I moan as we kiss. I love him....

An hour later Vic comes. Trevor and I both greet her with a hug. "Let's see the ring!" I say excitedly. "Okay!" She says and reveals a beautiful diamond ring. It's quite big and the diamond is in the shape of a circle. "Congratulations, beautiful girl!" says Trevor taking Victoria by the hand and turns her round. I smile and laugh. Then Trevor whispers in my ear, "But you're 100 times more..."

Trevor and Victoria go through to the family room and I switch on Taylor Swifts 'Wildest Dreams'. I lay the table then join them. Victoria looks lovely, she's wearing a loose knitted cream top/dress, without any trousers. The top/dress slips of one shoulder and sits on her arm. Her blonde hair is crimped and she's wearing light pink lip-gloss, black eyeliner, white eye-shadow, concealer and mascara. And she's glowing with pride and happiness. I smile at her and sit next to Trevor. Trevor drapes his arm over me and leans back on the couch. "So, How's Brandon? How did he propose?" I say excitedly, wanting all the latest gossip.

"Ok, Ok!" she laughs. "He's good. Basically we were watching the sun go down from a cliff and we were leaning back with his arm round me and suddenly the vision of the sunset is blocked by his hand holding a ring box open with a beautiful ring inside. I gasped and said yes when he asked me.

He said: 'I'm so lucky but why would a girl like you ever want to marry, or even talk to, a guy like me?' and I said 'Why not?!' It was the most romantic moment! And then we collapsed on the ground kissing madly, afterwards we just stared up at the dark night sky with my legs and arms wrapped round him!" she tells us both as I listen in happiness.

"Oh my word! That's so cute! Congrats!" I say again.

"Yeah, great, lovely, romantic, whatever!" says Trevor, obviously tired of the girls discussing their sappy love stories! Vic and I glance at each-other then burst out laughing. Then we all have dinner and Vic leaves after a 'packeted' starbucks coffee, a chat about me quitting and a visit to see Riley and put her to off to sleep.

Later I check on Riley, who's sleeping soundly. Then Trevor goes to bed. Afterwards I call Jennie and we talk about married life, having children and just life in general! Tristan, Jennie's son is 1 year old! Then I go upstairs to go to bed.

Trevor

I pretend to be asleep as Brit gets
ready and once she's ready and in
my arms I grab her arm and pull
her in. She giggles and says, "Trevor!
Your so naughty!" Then our lips lock
and she presses her hands against
my chest as she sits on my stomach.
We kiss for a solid 3 minutes then
break apart, breathing heavily. We
then just hug for ages, with Brittany

next to me, her arms and legs wrapped round me as we close our eyes and eventually fall asleep. We wake suddenly at 6am in the morning to Riley's crying.

"I'll go." Says Brittany tiredly.

Brittany

Just as I'm half way down the corridor to Riley's bedroom, my stomach gives a sudden lurch and I rush to the bathroom. I get down on my hands and knees as I'm sick in the toilet. What's going on? I don't feel good, probably something funny in that noodle soup last night. Oh goodness, I hope Vic and Trev don't have it too. I wash my face then continue down the corridor to Riley's room. Riley stops yelling/crying as soon as I walk into the room. She's standing on her feet with her small hands leaning on the crib side. She bounces up and down and smiles as I walk over.

"Good morning Riles! Shall we get ready?!" I ask,

"Yes, mommy, me, readdddddyyyyyyy! NOOOOOOWWWWW" She shouts

surprisingly demandingly. I take her through to the bathroom and run a bath. Then I take off Riley's clothes and lift her in. She splashes about as I kneel at the side. Afterwards I pull her out and I dry her with her butterfly towel hoodie. Then I brush her hair and tie it up in two little pigtails, as usual. Then she helps me choose out some grey toddler jeans with sparkles and a blue, green and white frilly tartan top and finally a matching tartan bow, which I clip into her hair. With her ready it's my turn. I shower, unfortunately with several breaks to be sick. Then I put on my usual makeup and curl my smoky blonde hair at the front. Afterwards I put on a stylish baggy brown cream top and blue jeans. I add some brown sandals to complete the look. Then I go downstairs to Trevor and Riley at the breakfast table. I smile at Riley as she sits in her high chair swinging her legs. I pour some frosties into a bowl and hand her them.

"Sweetheart, are you ok? You look a bit pale." Asks Trevor, obviously concerned.

"Yeah, yeah, I'm fine! Just been a bit sick, that's all! It must be something I ate. Hope you don't get it too." I say as cheerily as I can.

"Ok, but I better go. I can be home in 20 minutes if I need to! 'K baby?" he asks me, and I feel a wave of relief wash over me as I hear that he'll come home if I need him. Of course I knew he would but just to hear him say it makes me feel even more relieved.

"Ok, Love you, babe!" I say as I give him a kiss.

"Bwye Bwye dadwa!" says Riley sweetly as she waves at him.

"Bye sweetheart! Daddy'll see you later!" Says Trevor as he gives her a kiss on the cheek. "Bye baby girl! See you later! Love ya!" He says cheekily to me as he kisses me again. Then, after picking up his bags, he's gone. I wave and so does Riley, as I hold her on the kitchen cabinet so she can see through the window. He waves back and blows a kiss.

"Right! Let's put on the TV and watch 'The Next Step!'" I suggest and she immediately runs through to the family room and jumps on the couch, getting herself all comfy! I smile and bomb onto the couch with her, crossing my legs. I tickle her as she giggles hysterically. Then I grab the remote and switch on the TV. I turn it to saved shows. I click on 'The Next Step! - season 8'. Its the last season, and we begin watching, with Riley on my knee and the TNS blanket draped over us both. Riley has still not worked out that Riley

and James on TV, the pair of us, are

her mummy and daddy!

 "Me! Riley!" She says excitedly,

pointing at the TV as I appear on

screen. I just laugh. Then James

appears and.... "DADDY!" says Riley,

pointing at the screen as Trevor

appears on screen. I gasp, she

recognized him.

I clap, "Yes, that's daddy!" I say. I

feel a bit jealous that she recognized

him, but I guess I look more different, whereas Trevor looks the same. When suddenly..... "Mommy!" she says. As she jumps on my knee, making me jump. I just stare. She recognized me! AT LAST!

"Yes! That's mommy! That's me!" I say excitedly, "YES! YES! THAT'S RIGHT! Well done sweetie!" I praise her. Then she's on a role...

"Lamar! Victovia! Tateeta! Fordan! Logaaaannn!" She says proudly as everyone appears on screen and I'm so happy I start jumping up and down on the couch! "Yes! Yes! Yes!" I say and clap. Then still on cloud 9, I sit down and TRY to calm down. I'm so proud of my little girl! When that episodes over, Riley yawns and rubs her eyes. I smile with pride. Then I pick her up and sit her on my hip as I carry her to her room By the time I get there she's fallen asleep. So I lay her in her crib, put the blanket over

her and lean in to kiss her head. I
close the curtains and smile again as
I switch the lights off and close the
door. Then just as I'm out of the
room I feel another lurch and run to
the bathroom to be sick. Just as I
stand back up from the toilet I think
about a possibility......Wait a minute!
I couldn't be.....no that's
impossible.......but could it be?. I
suddenly realise and just to make

sure I text Samantha, my fingers

fumbling over the words:
SNS! Could you run an errand for me big
sis? Bxx

A minute later a reply appears:
Sure! What's happening? Are u ok? End of
conversation! I'm coming!

See! I have the best sister ever!

Twenty minutes later she arrives. I

hear the doorbell ring and answer it

quickly so it doesn't wake Riley.

"Hey! You ok?" She asks as soon as

the doors open.

"Yes! Fine! Come in!" I say quickly, before she gets any ideas. I take her through to the family room and we sit with coffees.

"So?...." she asks.

"Sis, I think I'm pregnant....." I say nervously, waiting for her surprised reaction. But she just sits there calmly. "Sis! Say something!" I say desperately.

"I did have a suspicion so I brought the kit with me!" she answers, again super-freakily calmly. I am so surprised, it takes me a minute to realize my mouth is hanging open. I immediately close it when I realize. "Let's take the test.....come on!" she says calmly as she gets up and begins walking up the stairs. I silently follow her. Then it hits me why she's so calm, she's gone through the shock 2 times already, she has 2 kids. I don't know why I didn't realize before! She ushers me into the bathroom as soon as we get

upstairs and hands me a pregnancy

pot and stick. I close the door and

take 2 tests, just to be sure.

Afterwards, Samantha and I make

small talk, still Samantha remains

calm. After 15 minutes of nerves I

slowly walk back into the bathroom

and take a deep anxious breath

before turning the test over. It has

two lines, What does that mean? I

check the box and it says it means

'Yes, you are pregnant, congratulations'.

Oh goodness, no, no! Samantha's sitting patiently on the bed outside, I glance at her nervously. Then turn the other one over, again two lines! I'm pregnant! It's official! Twice!!! Now I'm actually nervously excited. A little sibling for Riley! "Sam?!" I call, "Yeah?!" she says, walking through calmly. I glance at her anxiously again as she surveys the tests. "Congrats!" She says excitedly

and we hug then after another

coffee she leaves.

Trevor

Finally I get home and dump my bags. Brit comes running through and hugs my sweaty body (sweaty from dancing) and lifts her feet off the ground, my neck supporting her.

"Hey baby girl..." I whisper in her ear.

"Honey, I need to talk to you." She says.

"Sure!" I say, "I'll just shower and change......" I say as I begin walking to the stairs but she grabs my arm, "Now!" she says and as I turn to see her she's doing her pleading puppy dog eyes, I can never resist those big chocolaty brown eyes. So I give in and walk through to the family room with her. I sit on the couch and she sits on my knee.

"What?" I ask immediately.

"You'll need this first!" she says calmly as she puts her finger to my lips to hush me. Then she leans in and she kisses me, I return the kiss forcefully. We do this for several minutes then break apart. I look at her gorgeous face as she stares at me.

"You're gorgeous..." I say,

"You're gorgeous too!" she answers. Then we just sit staring at each-other for what seems like ages.

"Babe, I need to tell you this.....I'm pregnant." She says.

I just stare at her. "What!? Wow! I.......ummm...." I stutter. She sits on my knee staring into my brown eyes nervously. "When did you....." I ask. "Just today......Sam came over......She was so helpful and calm......I must of conceived a month and a half ago. You know....." she tells me quietly. Suddenly I process this. She's pregnant! What's wrong with me?

Riley will be a big sister!

"Sweetheart! This...This is great,

another baby! WOW!" I enthuse

happily.

"Re...,really?!" she says with a spring

of hope.

"Yes! I love you!" I say and kiss her

gently on the lips as I take her of the

sofa and lift her up into my arms.

Later, once we've calmed down we're

just sitting on the sofa with Brit on

my knee and we're just silent, a

happy silent. Brit's leaning her head against my shoulder. And we're just content.

Brittany

I snuggle into Trevor and smile. Life is good!

Later that day.......

Trevor's playing with Riley in her room. He was so pleased when he heard that Riley knew who everyone was in their roles in the show! I text the whole cast on group texting

saying:

Thought you'd all like to know that Trev
and I are expecting another arrival, A new
sibling for Riles!
Bxx

I immediately get responses. Vic

already knows, she's my bestie, I

texted her an hour after I told Trev.

Tav texts:

Oh my word ya'll! You go girl! Congrats!
Tavxx

Jordan texts:

Ahhhhhhhhh! Amazing! CONGRATS!

Vic texts:

Yes! Amazing right!

Lamar texts:

Yes! Another little minion for my army of pranksters! Feeling pumped!

I laugh, Lamar LOVES Riley.

Isaac texts:

WOW! Congrats dudet and of course, Trevor my man! Just told Ricky, She offers to babysit Riley and her sibling!

I laugh, Ricky is so nice, and pretty! She's Isaac's girlfriend. Trevor told me that Isaac told him that Isaac's planning to propose next year. They ARE perfect for each-other! I then switch off my phone and since it's 10pm, I go to bed. My first pregnancy exam's tomorrow, I don't

like the unltrasound........

8 months later......

With one month to go till Julie

Amelie's birth (we found out the sex,

a girl, and named her Julie Amelie.

Julie for short.) I'm getting nervous.

Right now I'm sleeping in bed, well I

say sleeping, I'm lying wide awake.

Suddenly I feel a punch in my stomach and give a yelp. Then the LIGHTS GO OUT!

Trevor

I look nervously down at my wife as we shoot down the road in an ambulance. She looks peaceful but she's unconscious. She's having a threatened abortion and if we don't get the baby out in the next 20 minutes there is a risk that she and the baby will die. A single tear slides down my cheek, this isn't like me. I wipe it away and clasp her hand.

"Brittany! Don't leave me. I need you. We need you!" I cry to her as I rest my head against her breast.

"You won't..." comes a soft tired voice. I immediately jolt up in surprise and look deeply into her eyes.

"We need to get the baby out." I tell her, "I can't lose you!"

"You won't, I'll see you soon." She says calmly, then closes her eyes again.

A few hours later......

Brittany is resting in the hospital bed with a drip. She even manages to rock in a hospital gown! Suddenly her head moves and I look hopefully at her. She tiredly opens her eyes and I smile with relief.

"Hi...." she croaks, smiling, I laugh gently,

"Hi...." I say as I stroke her cheek. I kiss her gently and slowly. When we pull apart she tries to sit up but I push her down. "Rest," I whisper but she forcefully sits up. How, when she's so ill is she so gorgeous?

"The baby!" she suddenly says alarmed, "Did I lose it? Please no!"

"No, no. Julie, our little girl! She's still a month premature though, she's in the NICU." I tell her gently.

"Can....Can I see her?" Brit asks

nervously.

"I'll check with the doc. Be back in a

minute!" I say and hop up.

Brittany

A few minutes later....

The doctor checks a few things then releases the drip from my arm and helps me out of bed into the wheel chair. The doctor pushes me through long hospital corridors smelling of disinfectant while Trevor holds my hand and squeezes it. Finally we get to a small door and

the doctor scans his pass. I can't
quite believe it when I'm taken into a
small room within NICU. A warm
tear slides down my cheek as I see
my daughter. She has fair blondie-
brownie hair and she's gorgeous
and adorable and so small..... The
doctor presses a few buttons then he
takes her out. He hands me her
and....wow......she's tiny! She has only
a diaper and socks on. She finds the
room so cold after being in the

NICU so she curls her tiny red

mottled newborn body up onto me.

"Can.....Can I feed her?" I ask

anxiously.

"Well, you are in a weak condition,

and its before Julie was due so your

milk might not be processing

properly." He answers carefully and

my face falls, "But you can certainly

try!" he adds. I look at Trevor and he

jumps up from the seat he's sitting

on and gently takes Julie from me, it

doesn't feel right! I look at the

doctor as I begin to undo my gown

and he turns round instinctively.

Trevor carefully hands Julie back

and I put her near my breast and

she suckles, I smile.

2 weeks later......

Finally today is the day we get to

take Julie home! I have had to live in

hospital the last two weeks as well

because of my condition but I'm fine now. Julie is still tiny and hasn't grown at all but her heart rate is better and they are allowing us to take her home! Frank called and we've forgiven each other and I'm starting work again soon but he understands that family comes first! I'm wearing a thin black hoodie with a white and pink sequin loose top underneath and my thin soft smoky dyed (different shades of blonde that blend) hair is tied up in a kind of cute pop out pony-tail at the back with loose strands at the front. I'm also wearing Grey scruffy ripped jeans and black converse. I buckle Julie's tiny body into her car seat and kiss her tiny head. I close the door and go round the front of the car, get in, do my seat belt and close the door. Trevor smiles at me as I glance at him, I smile back. He grabs my hand and squeezes it tightly, the way he does. He begins driving and I look back at Julie as she sleeps. She has beautiful blue eyes (unusual in our family) and she's so good and quiet, different from her sister. She's wearing a cute little white dress with brownish cream, black and grey giraffe shadows on it, she's also wearing some tiny little fluffy white baby booties. "You're going to meet your big sister for the first time!" I tell her excitedly. Because Julie was

in the NICU, we've not allowed Riley
to visit her. I've face-timed Riley
every day and she's so excited, my
mum's been taking care of her. And
Vic's getting married in a week plus
I'm her bridesmaid and Riley's her
flower-girl! Finally we pull into our
drive and Riley immediately appears
on the doorstep with my mum
behind her. I wave and Riley waves
excitedly back while using her other
hand to suck her thumb. She's

wearing a Yellow dress, shiny yellow pumps and a large yellow button clip. Looking the part and cute at that! I get out of the car and run to hug her. "Sweetie, mommy's missed you!" I tell her happily as I lift her up. Trevor walks over and takes her out of my arms to give her a hug.

"SISTA!" Riley says excitedly as she points at the car.

"Yes sweetheart! Your sister's in the car." I tell her,

"Shall mommy get her?" Trevor asks her.

"Yes!" says Riley clapping her hands.

So I walk over the car, open the door and unbuckle Julie's car seat. Then I gently take her out and hold her tiny body. I close the door and walk back over. Riley stares in awe. I smile.

"Want to hold her?" I ask.

"YES! YES! YES!" Riley screams.

"Ohhkkkk...." I laugh. Then I

carefully carry Julie inside while

Trevor carries Riley.

"She's beautiful...They both are! You

did well, honey." Says my mum

gently .

"I know, thanks Mum." I say

smiling. Riley sits on the sofa and I

carefully hand her Julie while my

mum supports Julie's head. I stand

back and look at Trevor. He tucks

my loose strands of hair from my

pop out pony-tail at the front

behind my ear and we kiss. Life is good!

Trevor

Ok, so Riley wasn't quite 3 years old!

But life is good!

A couple of years later......

It's 2 years later and Riley's 4 years old while Julie's 2 years old. Two weeks ago Brit gave birth to our first son, James Alec. James is named after my old role in TNS. He has light blonde hair and chocolatey brown eyes like Brit and I. Riley has short brown tightly bobbed hair and a short fringe which she suits and makes her even more gorgeous. Julie has long wavy soft silvery blonde hair with a tint of brown (showing it'll probably turn brown when she's older), outdoor pink cheeks and oddly (unlike the rest of the family) bright blue eyes-she is also gorgeous. Julie has a blue bird hair slide that she loves and always keeps in her hair, even at night. All my children are gorgeous and beautiful. James is adorable. Riley quit ballet and is now playing violin while Julie's dancing hip hop and ballet. Vic had her first daughter 2 days ago named Belle. And me and Brit are going away on a luxury holiday together next month to Banff in the Rockies. Brit is wearing a long sleeved white lace crop top with a hood with blue jeans and caramel brown fluffy Uggs. Brit and I are currently snuggling up on the sofa while Riley and Julie sleep. James is nestled in Brits arms, swaddled up in a cosy blue blanket with his tiny precious hands sticking out. She strokes each of his tiny mottled fingers and smiles. She tucks a strand of her smoky blonde hair behind her ear and looks at me.

"What?" she asks, embarrassed.

"You're just....gorgeous...." I tell her gently. She leans into look at me.

"I love you." She says, "

I love you just as much times a million..." I tell her and we kiss with James between us, sleeping.

Dedicated to Brittany Raymond, Trevor Tordjman, Victoria Baldesarra, The Next Step cast and crew, my family and friends and Butternut my doggy!

The End!

50903853R00054

Made in the USA
Charleston, SC
10 January 2016